Grundo Springtime Singtime

There's lots of fun in this
sing-along festival of songs.

Story by:
Will Ryan

Illustrated by:
David High
Russell Hicks
Theresa Mazurek
Allyn Conley/Gorniak
Julie Armstrong

WORLDS OF WONDER™

Grubby™ Newton Gimmick™ Princess Aruzia™ Leota™ Wooly What's-It™ Prince Arin™ Fobs™

Page 1

"Spring Has Sprung"

The weather's so much better now. I'll put away my sweater now.

They make you chuckle.
They make you giggle.

It's the oddest food I've ever seen. It's lumpy and it's sticky.

"A Happy Sing-Along Song"

You never know when a
wish will come true.